SONA SHARMA
WISH ME LUCK

CHITRA SOUNDAR

Illustrated by JEN KHATUN

WALKER BOOKS

TO MY DAD, WHO WISHED ON LUCKY CHARMS
AND THEN WORKED HARD TO MAKE HIS
WISHES (AND MINE) COME TRUE

First published in the UK 2023 by Walker Books Ltd
87 Vauxhall Walk, London SE11 5HJ

2 4 6 8 10 9 7 5 3 1

Text © 2023 Chitra Soundar
Illustrations © 2023 Jen Khatun

The right of Chitra Soundar and Jen Khatun to be identified as
author and illustrator respectively of this work has been asserted in
accordance with the Copyright, Designs and Patents Act 1988

This book has been typeset in Alegreya

Printed and bound by CPI Group (UK) Ltd, Croydon CR0 4YY

British Library Cataloguing in Publication Data:
a catalogue record for this book is available from the British Library

ISBN 978-1-5295-0480-4

MIX
Paper | Supporting
responsible forestry
FSC® C171272

www.walker.co.uk

CONTENTS

BREAKING EXCITEMENT

Sona Sharma lives in a large joint family
full of happy people who argue sometimes.
Relatives come unannounced, the phone
rings often and everyone is always welcome
whatever the time.

These are Sona's people:

Amma – Sona's mum. She is a music teacher and singer. She's always humming a song or listening to music.

Appa – Sona's dad. He works with computers all day and sometimes at night too.

Minmini – Minmini means "firefly", and she is Sona's baby sister who is almost one.

Thatha – Sona's grandfather. He knows a lot of things. And when he doesn't know about something, he tells a story about something else.

Paatti – Sona's grandmother. She makes the best sweets in the whole world. She always laughs at Thatha's jokes.

The President – Sona's other grandmother. Sona doesn't know her real name. The President used to be the president of some college, so everyone calls her that still. She lives in the only orange house in the entire neighbourhood, called The Orange.

Joy and Renu – Sona's friends from school. They live a street away and go to school with Sona in an auto-rickshaw.

Mullai – Sona's auto-rickshaw driver. She picks up Sona, Joy and Renu in that order, to drop off at school. In the evening, she takes them home – Renu first, Joy next and Sona last. She's never late and recites a lot of Tamil poetry.

Miss Rao – Sona, Joy and Renu's class teacher. She is kind, funny and strict all at the same time. Sona and her friends hope she'll be their teacher for ever.

Elephant – Sona's best friend. He fits perfectly in Sona's toy bag and her cuddly chair and next to her on her pillow. Sona never goes anywhere without him, except, of course, to school.

That Friday morning, when Sona came down from her room to get breakfast, she couldn't contain her excitement.

"It's the last day of school," she said to Elephant.

"For ever?" asked Elephant.

"Not for ever, silly," said Sona. "The last day before our mid-term break. Nine whole days."

"What will we do for nine whole days at home?" asked Elephant.

"Good question, Elephant," said Sona, and decided to make a list of things she could do during the break.

1. Go on an adventure.
2. Write a book with lots of pictures in it.

"Will I be in it?" asked Elephant.

"Absolutely," said Sona. "All my books will have elephants in them."

3. Go to a museum.
4. Spend time with my friends.
5. Play board games.

Sona put her list aside and ran downstairs when she heard Mullai honk. Soon they were off to school.

"Do you have any big plans for the break, girls?" asked Mullai, as they zoomed along.

"I'm making a list," said Sona.

"I'm going to read zillions of books," said Joy.

"I'm going to visit my grandparents," said Renu.

"Here we are," said Mullai, pulling up in front of the school. "Enjoy your last day of term."

The whole school was extra noisy during assembly and still their principal, Mrs Girija Shekar, didn't tell them off even once.

There were no more lessons to do. On the last day of term, they read stories in the library, had an extra art session and sang funny songs in Music class.

When it was hometime, Renu sang, "Holiday, holiday, time to go away..."

"Holiday, holiday, loads of time to play," finished Sona.

Miss Rao clapped her hands to get their attention. "I know you're all excited to get started on your break," she said. "But I have an important announcement to make."

"Please don't give us holiday homework," said Joy. "I want to read a zillion books."

"No holiday homework," said Miss Rao. "It's a happy announcement."

"Tell us, Miss," said Sona.

"I'm getting married," said Miss Rao. "Next Thursday."

"Married?" Renu exclaimed.

"That's only six days away," said Joy, counting it out on her fingers.

"Can we come to the wedding?" asked Sona.

"Yes, of course," said Miss Rao. "I'll be sending invitations to your parents. Keep a lookout for the post."

That evening, when Sona, Joy and Renu got into the auto-rickshaw, their excitement had shifted from what to do in the break to what dresses they should wear for Miss Rao's wedding.

"Should we go in matching skirts and blouses?" asked Sona.

"That's a great idea," said Joy.

Renu was quiet.

"What's wrong?" asked Sona.

"I hope we return from our village in time for the wedding."

"You've got to be there," said Joy. "For Miss Rao's sake."

As they turned from the busy road into a quiet street, Mullai asked, "So do you know if Miss Rao is coming back after her wedding?"

"Coming back where?" asked Sona.

"To school," said Mullai. "What if her husband is from another city? She'll have to go and live with him."

Sona looked at Joy and Renu in shock. Could that happen? They had never imagined going to school without Miss Rao as their teacher.

For the rest of the ride home, Sona and her friends held hands.

"I think she'll be back," whispered Sona, emphatically.

"I'm not sure," said Joy. "My cousin got married and she had to move to England to be with her husband."

"My aunt came from Kerala when she married my uncle," said Renu. "She only visits her home town once a year."

Oh no! They couldn't even ask Miss Rao about it because the next time they would see her would be on her wedding day and that might be too late.

EIGHT FOR A WISH

The next morning when Sona woke up, the
first thing she remembered was Miss Rao's
wedding. What if Miss Rao never came back to
teach their class?

She ran downstairs with Elephant to check
the letter box.

"The postman will be here only after eleven a.m.," said Thatha, who was sitting in the front room with his newspaper and a steel tumbler full of coffee.

"Oh!"

"Anything special you're expecting?" asked Thatha. "Letter from a pen friend?"

"What's a pen friend?" asked Sona.

"A friend you talk to only through letters," said Thatha. "Your appa used to have a few pen friends. He'd wait by the letter box every Saturday hoping for a letter from one of them."

"My friends live in the neighbourhood," said Sona, "and they have phones. I can just call them."

Thatha chuckled as he went back to his newspaper.

Sona ran to find Amma, who was at the dining table, feeding Baby Minmini.

"Can I call Joy and Renu to come over?" she asked.

"Good morning to you too, my lovely," said Amma. "Sure! After you've finished your breakfast."

"And here is your breakfast," Paatti said, coming out with a plate full of idlies with sambhar on the side.

"Thank you, Paatti," said Sona as she sat down next to Amma at the table. She ate without looking up once. She didn't talk or move her food around or even stop to explain something interesting with her mouth full.

"Finished!" she declared, getting up from the table. "Can I call my friends now? Please."

Amma smiled and nodded as she played "here comes the food plane" with Minmini.

"Are you OK?" asked Elephant. "You've never eaten this fast."

"I'm not OK," said Sona to Elephant. "Miss Rao might never come back and I'm in a panic."

"But you *love* Miss Rao!" said Elephant.

"I know!" said Sona.

But Renu's phone kept ringing and ringing. Ah! Sona remembered Renu was away for a couple of days. She called Joy.

"I'm coming right away," said Joy.

Joy arrived singing a song that Sona had never heard before.

"One for sorrow,
Two for joy,
Three for a girl,
Four for a boy,

Five for silver,
Six for gold,
Seven for a secret, never to be told.
Eight for a wish,
Nine for a kiss,
Ten a surprise you should be careful not to miss."

"What's that song?" asked Sona.

"My cousin in England taught it to me," said Joy. "If you spot two magpies, they will bring you joy."

"If I ever see eight magpies together, I'll wish that Miss Rao will always be our teacher," said Sona.

"Me too," said Joy.

"But there are hardly any magpies in India," said Sona. "Our wish might never come true."

"My cousin said we could spot ravens instead of magpies."

Sona brightened up. "Let's go to the roof terrace," she said. "Ravens come to our mango tree."

Sona, Joy and Elephant sat on the bench on the terrace, under the mango tree's shade, looking

up into the branches. Crows cawed. But no
ravens yet.

"Careful not to spot a single raven," said Joy.
"One is for sorrow!"

They waited and waited. Joy was bored. Sona
was bored. Elephant was bored. Thatha came to
the roof terrace to check on them.

"Something wrong?" asked Thatha. "Why are
you sitting here doing nothing?"

"We're waiting for ravens," said Sona.

"But we can't find any," said Joy.

"Is it a science project or something?" asked Thatha.

Joy sang the song for Thatha. "We need to spot eight ravens," she said.

"To make a wish," said Sona.

"Oh! I see," he said. "Did you try feeding them?"

Sona jumped up and hugged Thatha. "You're the cleverest thatha I have."

"I'm your only thatha," he replied with a chuckle, as he followed them downstairs.

Sona and Joy brought a cup of steamed rice and scattered it on the terrace floor for the birds. First one crow turned up. But instead of eating, he called his friends. Soon more crows arrived, and some ravens too.

Sona and Joy couldn't contain their excitement. They counted the ravens. One, two, three, four, five, six!

"Six for gold!" shouted Joy.

"I'm already gold," said Sona, "'Sona' means 'gold'. I need eight ravens to make my wish."

Crows came in droves. Squirrels tried to sneak off with the rice. But eight ravens never came together.

"So that didn't work," said Joy.

But Sona wasn't ready to give up. "We need to find more lucky charms," she said.

After Thatha took Joy home, Sona too got busy looking for lucky charms. "Come on, Elephant," she said. "We've work to do."

"Elephants don't do work," Elephant replied. "Especially during the holidays."

"Elephants help their friends, right?" asked Sona.

"Yup! Always."

Sona giggled and hugged Elephant, as she began her quest for lucky charms.

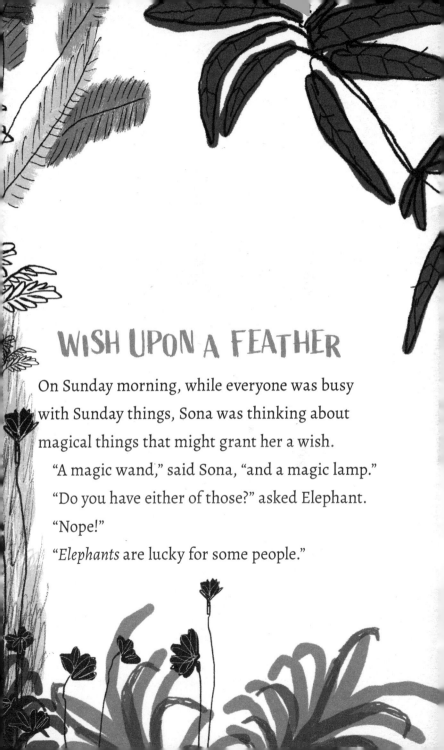

WISH UPON A FEATHER

On Sunday morning, while everyone was busy with Sunday things, Sona was thinking about magical things that might grant her a wish.

"A magic wand," said Sona, "and a magic lamp."

"Do you have either of those?" asked Elephant.

"Nope!"

"*Elephants* are lucky for some people."

"That's true," said Sona. "But can you grant me a wish?"

"Nope!"

"Hmm," said Sona. Appa was going out somewhere. "Bye, Sona," he called.

"Oh, Appa, wait!" shouted Sona.

"Argh! Don't call someone when they are leaving," cried Paatti. "That's bad luck."

"But I want to ask him about his good luck charms!"

Appa laughed. "My good luck charms are you, my superstar, and your sister, Minmini, the little star."

After Appa left, Paatti said, "Your appa doesn't believe in good luck charms. But your aunty Lini – she had a good luck charm when she was your age."

"Really?"

Paatti clicked her tongue and went to the bookshelf. She moved the books around, then said, "There it is!"

Sona rushed to Paatti's side. "Show me, show me! What is it?"

It was a hardbound book with a red cover. Paatti opened the centre page. Sona gasped. Inside was a perfect peacock feather. The eye in the middle of the feather glimmered in the sunlight.

"Lini used to whisper her wishes to this peacock feather," said Paatti, "and close the book. She believed it made her wishes come true."

Sona's eyes sparkled with excitement. Maybe this peacock feather would make Miss Rao come back to their class!

"Will Aunty Lini mind if I use it?" asked Sona.

"Of course not," said Paatti. "You can have it."

Sona took the book back to her room.

"This peacock feather might grant my wish to keep Miss Rao," she told Elephant.

"Even if she has to go and live somewhere else?" asked Elephant.

"Hmm," said Sona.

"Poor Miss Rao," said Elephant. "It will be hard for her to come to school every day from another city."

Sona turned to look at Elephant strangely. "It won't be hard," she said. "She loves us more. A lot more."

Sona opened the book and gently picked up the

feather in her hand. "Please make Miss Rao come back to teach our class after the wedding," she whispered softly, then put the feather carefully back into the book and closed it.

That night, Sona's dreams were full of ravens and peacocks, dancing in the forest.

FORTUNE FAVOURS
THE BRAVE

The next morning, right after breakfast, the phone rang.

"Miss Sona Sharma," called Thatha. "Phone call for you."

Elephant giggled. "That's funny," he said.

"It's not funny," said Sona. "That's my full name."

It was Renu. "I'm back from the village," she said. "Joy told me all about the ravens and asked me to find lucky charms. I found a lucky thing in the village."

"What is it?" asked Sona.

"Joy and I are coming over to show it to you," said Renu.

When Joy and Renu peeped into Sona's room, Elephant was fast asleep. Sona was colouring in her drawings of a peacock feather.

"Oh wow! That's beautiful," said Renu.

"Yes, I made a wish on a peacock feather," said Sona. "Aunty Lini used to do that."

"Oh! So, you don't want the lucky charm I brought?" Renu asked, her smile disappearing.

"We still need it!" replied Sona. "We need all the luck we can get."

"Show us your lucky thing," said Joy. "What is it?"

Renu pulled out a little cloth pouch from her pocket. She emptied its contents out on top of a book. Three red beads.

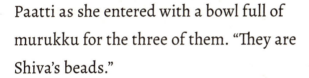

"Those look like Rudraksha beads," said Paatti as she entered with a bowl full of murukku for the three of them. "They are Shiva's beads."

"They are Renu's," said Joy.

Sona giggled. "She meant Shiva, the god who destroys evil. He's a Hindu god with a trident who lives on a mountain peak called Kailash."

"That's right," said Paatti.

"Is there a story about the beads?" asked Sona.

"We love stories," said Renu. "Please tell us."

Paatti sat on the bed next to them and cleared her throat. Sona, Elephant, Joy and Renu huddled around to listen.

"Lord Shiva, the destroyer of evil, was meditating on Mount Kailash with his eyes closed. He meditated for hundreds of years. He meditated as the snow melted and re-formed. He meditated as the Earth shook and oceans bubbled.

"And then finally, one day, when he opened his eyes, two lotus-shaped tears fell from his eyes onto Earth. A tree sprouted on the spot where they fell. That tree is called the Rudraksha and the fruits that grow on this tree are called the Rudraksha beads."

When Paatti finished the story, Sona asked, "So, are they lucky?"

"They are used like rosary beads for meditating," said Paatti. "And yes, many people believe that they ward off evil."

"What does 'ward off evil' mean?" asked Renu.

"That if you keep the beads with you," said Paatti, "bad things will not happen to you."

Paatti hurried downstairs to get on with the cooking, while Sona and her friends munched on murukku.

"This is perfect," said Sona. "The peacock feather will grant my wish for Miss Rao to stay…"

"And the beads will stop bad things happening, like Miss Rao leaving," finished Renu.

"Fingers crossed," said Joy. And the three girls smiled at each other.

That night, when Amma came to wish her goodnight, Sona told her all about the peacock feather and the Rudraksha beads and Paatti's story.

"That's nice," said Amma. "Why do you want all these lucky charms?"

"That's a secret," said Sona. The wishes might not work if she told Amma.

"I see," said Amma. "As long as you don't wish for something impossible."

"Our wish is definitely possible," replied Sona.

"Fortune favours the brave, Sona," said Amma. "May your wishes come true."

"What does that mean?" asked Sona.

"It means, if you wish for something, go and make it happen," said Amma.

"How?" whispered Sona.

"Let me tell you about the time I entered a singing competition when I was in school," said Amma. "Mullai and I were going to sing a duet. We learned many songs. But Mullai didn't want to practise or sing in the competition.

She wanted to be playing cricket or basketball."

"What did you do?" asked Sona. "Did you make her sing?"

"Of course not," said Amma. "Mullai was happier on the playing fields than in the music room. But I loved singing. So, I sang in the competition on my own."

"Were you upset with Mullai?"

"I was a little bit disappointed," said Amma. "But I won the competition and then realized I wanted to be a singer when I grew up. And Mullai was there to cheer me on. And she still comes to many of my performances, doesn't she?"

Sona nodded.

"Fortune favours the brave," Amma repeated. "If you want something, go and make it happen. Don't worry about lucky charms and wishes. We must work hard to make our wishes come true. And if they don't, I'm always here to talk to you and hug you."

"Me too," whispered Elephant.

"Thank you," said Sona.

Thatha's "On Time Every Time" pendulum clock rang loudly downstairs.

"Now, go to sleep, Sona," said Amma, kissing Sona on the forehead. "Goodnight, wake up bright."

After Amma left the room, Sona lay in bed thinking.

"What are you thinking about?" asked Elephant.

"I have to be brave," said Sona, "and do brave things to make my wish come true."

"I'll be brave with you," said Elephant.

"Thank you," whispered Sona, closing her eyes.

A PLAN OF ACTION

On Tuesday morning, Sona was waiting by the front gate when Appa came looking for her.

"What are you doing here?" he asked. "It's my day off today and I thought we could go to a museum or something?"

"That was on your holiday list," Elephant reminded Sona.

"I'm waiting for the postman," Sona told Appa.

Right on cue, "Post!" cried a voice. The letter box rattled. Appa opened the box and pulled out an envelope.

"A wedding invitation," he said. "Wonder whose it is..."

"It's for me," cried Sona as she grabbed it out of Appa's hands and ran inside.

"It's got my name on it," said Appa, chasing after her.

Elephant giggled in Sona's hands. He hadn't played tag with Sona and Appa in a long time.

Sona leaped onto the sofa and opened the invitation.

"Hey, it says Gopinath Sharma on the front!"

"No, it says Mrs & Mr Gopinath Sharma and

family," said Sona. "I'm your family, so I'm allowed to open it. It's Miss Rao's wedding anyway."

"Oh! I see!" said Appa.

There were two cards inside the envelope.

"So, this is for the

traditional wedding
ceremony in the
morning," said Appa,
pointing to the yellow
one. "This blue card is for
the reception in the evening.
We're invited to both."

Appa pointed out the groom's name on the
invitation. "Balaji, that's the name of the groom."

"Who are they?" asked Sona, pointing to the
names at the bottom of the invitation.

"These are Miss Rao's parents," said Appa,
"and those are Balaji's parents."

Appa read out the cities printed below their
names. It said "Chennai" under the names of
Miss Rao's parents. But on the groom's side, it
said "Vijayawada".

Sona gasped. "Where is Vijayawada?" she
asked. "Not in Chennai, right?"

"Nope! It's far away," said Appa.

"Can you show it to me on the map?" asked
Sona.

Appa opened his tablet and pointed at Vijayawada on the map. "It is ... four hundred and fifty-five kilometres away," he said.

"That's very far, right?" asked Sona. "Miss Rao can't come to school from there every day."

"Nope!"

Sona's worst fears were coming true.

DING-DONG!

The doorbell rang. The President walked in, carrying a big bunch of bananas.

"How lovely," said Elephant. "She has brought bananas for me."

"Good morning, Sona and Gopi," said the President. "Where are Nidhi and Minmini?"

"Good morning," said Appa. "Nidhi has just gone to the shops. She'll be back soon."

Sona was still staring at the map on the tablet.

"Is that Miss Rao's wedding invitation?" asked

the President. "Mine just came in the post too."

"Yup!" said Appa. "We're not very happy about it. We think Miss Rao might be moving to Vijayawada."

"Oh! That explains it," said the President.

Sona shot out of her seat in shock. "Explains what?" she demanded.

"Miss Rao said that instead of gifts, we should send money to an education charity called VidyaDaan," the President explained. "It's written on the back of the blue card."

Sona grabbed the blue card and turned it over. The President was right.

"What does that mean?" asked Sona.

"Maybe she's moving to Vijayawada and she doesn't want to carry lots of wedding gifts."

"So, she's really moving to Vijayawada?"

"Maybe," said the President. "With most weddings, the woman moves to the husband's city."

This was bad, thought Sona. Her peacock feather wish wasn't working. The red Rudraksha beads weren't stopping bad things from happening.

Sona's eyes filled with tears.

"What's wrong, Sona?" asked the President, as she pulled Sona close.

"If Miss Rao moves to Vijayawada, she won't be our teacher any more," said Sona. "I don't want a new teacher. What if the new teacher is horrible?"

"What if your new teacher is even lovelier than Miss Rao?" asked the President.

"It doesn't matter," said Sona. "I want Miss Rao. We love Miss Rao."

"If you love her, don't you want her to be happy?" asked the President. "If she wants to be with her husband in Vijayawada, we should let her go, right?"

Sona couldn't stop her tears any more. This was impossible. The grown-ups were always doing things that she couldn't change.

"I can't stop her going, because she's a grown-up and I'm not," said Sona, between sobs.

"Even grown-ups can't stop some things from happening," said the President. "When my son, your uncle, Prasad wanted to go abroad to study, I didn't want him to go."

The President had tears in her eyes too. "I was his mum, a grown-up. But I didn't stop him, because I knew he really wanted to go and he would have been sad if he'd stayed back here just for me."

Sona reached out and hugged the President. For a long time.

"Psst!" said Elephant. "Are you going to be long? I'm getting a bit squashed here."

Sona sat back on the sofa, burying her face in Elephant's head.

"It'll all work out," said Appa. "Whatever happens we'll make the best of it, Sona."

Sona nodded. She understood that she should be happy for Miss Rao. So why did the whole thing make her feel so sad?

A WEDDING PETITION

After the President left, Appa didn't want to
sit around doing nothing. "Come on, Sona," he
called. "We're going to the Rail Museum. I think
you'll enjoy it."

"I'm sure I won't," said Sona.

"You love trains," Elephant reminded her.

"Not today," said Sona. She had to make a plan
to stop Miss Rao leaving. *Fortune favours the brave,*
she told herself.

"I'm the grown-up and I've decided we're going," said Appa. "Do you want to ask if Joy and Renu would like to come with us?"

The grown-ups are always deciding everything, thought Sona. *It's so unfair!* But the idea of going out with Joy and Renu cheered her up a little.

Appa called Joy and Renu's parents and Paatti packed a bag of snacks and soon they were off.

From the outside yard to the inside halls, the museum was full of trains; old trains, really old trains and toy trains. Sona and her friends ran about exploring everything.

Joy pointed at a sign. "Can we go on the joy ride?"

"Of course. We must take Joy on the joy ride!" said Appa, buying tickets for them.

After that ride on the mini train, the sun got too hot, so they went inside the building, to see the model trains.

"Do you think Miss Rao will go to Vijayawada on a train?" asked Sona.

"What's Vijayawada?" asked Renu.

"That's where Miss Rao's husband lives," said Sona. "I saw it on the invitation."

Overhearing them, a passing museum guide said, "It takes almost seven hours to get to Vijayawada by train."

"That's very far," said Sona.

"She couldn't come to school from there every day," said Renu.

"You mean she's really leaving us?" asked Joy.

"I think so," said Sona, explaining the note on the back of the invitation about no gifts.

Appa came over to break their huddle. "Come on, let's get something to eat."

The restaurant was a remodelled train carriage. When they were waiting in line to order lunch, Sona spotted a red box with the word "FEEDBACK" written on it.

"Appa, what's that?" asked Sona.

"If you don't like the food or the service,"

explained Appa, "you can write a letter and drop it in there."

"And they will read it?" asked Joy.

"That's the hope – that they read it and fix the problem," said Appa.

That gave Sona an idea. "*We* can write a complaint letter!" she whispered to her friends.

"About what?" asked Renu. "We haven't even tried the food yet."

"Not about the food," said Sona. "About Miss Rao leaving."

"Yes!" cried Joy. "There's an Ideas box next to the principal's office at school."

"But won't Mrs Shekar read it?" asked Renu. "I don't want to get into trouble."

Appa put their plates in front of them. "Attention, passengers!" he called. "Your food has been served."

"I'm so hungry," said Sona.

"Me too," said Joy.

"Me three," said Renu.

"Me four!" said Elephant.

As they ate, Appa told them about the factory next to the museum where the train carriages were made.

As soon as he got up to get some more chutney, Joy looked up and whispered, "How about we write the complaint letter and hand it to Miss Rao?"

"Ooh, on her wedding day?" asked Renu. "Isn't that a bit rude?"

"It's not rude," said Sona. "We'll write a polite and friendly letter. Actually, we can ask everyone in our class to write a letter."

Appa came back right at that moment.

"You mean like a petition?" he asked.

"What's a petition?" asked Renu.

"When many people want to complain about the same thing, they write one letter and everyone signs it," said Appa. "Who are you complaining about?"

No one replied.

"Sona, is this about Miss Rao's wedding?" asked Appa in a serious voice. "If Miss Rao is leaving, shouldn't you be making farewell cards for her? What is there to complain about?"

Still, no one said anything.

"You're not asking Miss Rao not to get married, are you?" asked Appa.

"We're not that selfish," said Joy.

"We're only asking her to be our teacher for ever and ever," said Sona.

"Ah. Maybe we should talk about this, girls," said Appa.

"Later!" said Sona. "We want to look at more trains."

On their walk to the next exhibit, Joy whispered, "Let's write the letter tomorrow."

"Yes, then we can get everyone to sign it at the wedding," said Sona.

"Then we can give it to Miss Rao!" whispered Renu.

With a good plan firmly in place, Sona felt as if a weight had been lifted off her shoulders.

"Let's enjoy the museum now," she said. "I love trains."

"I knew it," said Elephant.

On Wednesday morning, Joy and Renu arrived early to write the petition. But Amma and Paatti wanted to talk about something else first.

"Have you girls decided what to wear for the wedding?" asked Paatti.

"We should wear the same colours," said Renu. "Right?"

"Can we?" asked Sona, turning to Amma.

"I thought you might say that," said Amma. "I've had a chat with both your mums, Joy and Renu. The one outfit you all have is a forest-green skirt and a pink silk blouse."

"That's my favourite skirt," said Renu.

"That's settled then," said Amma.

After breakfast, they sat on Sona's bed to work on the petition. For the next hour or so, they took turns making suggestions. Renu checked spellings in the dictionary. Joy looked for some grown-up words in the thesaurus. Sona checked the punctuation. Finally, they decided that the letter was perfect.

> Dear Miss Rao,
>
> We're so happy that you're getting married. But we don't want you to go and live in Vijayawada because it's far away and you won't be able to come to school from there every day.
>
> Please can you stay here in Chennai? You could visit your husband during weekends and holidays. That way, we will always have you as our teacher.
>
> With lots of love and respect,

Elephant squinted over at the letter. "I think you're missing something," he whispered.

"Drawings," said Sona. She drew some flowers and heart symbols. Renu coloured them in. Joy wrote *Miss Rao* in 3-D lettering on the envelope.

"Don't forget to bring the letter with you tomorrow," said Renu. "And a pen, so everyone can sign it."

"I won't forget," said Sona.

That evening, Amma and Sona picked out bangles and earrings and a necklace and shoes to match her outfit, and Sona helped choose Minmini's outfit.

"Can I have a handbag too?" asked Sona.

"Whatever for?" asked Appa.

"It's a style thing," said Thatha. "You wouldn't know anything about it."

"Hey, I'm stylish," joked Appa, striking a pose like a movie star.

Everyone laughed. Amma was giggling the most.

"How about this one?" asked Paatti, bringing her a rectangular, gold-coloured handbag with a golden metal strap.

"It's perfect," said Sona.

JAGGERY AND CUMIN

On the morning of Miss Rao's wedding day, Sona got ready quickly. Weddings were very crowded, busy and noisy, so Elephant decided to stay at home.

"Will you be all right on your own?" asked Sona.

"Don't worry about me," said Elephant. "Just make sure Miss Rao doesn't leave. Don't forget the petition."

Sona put the petition and pen inside Paatti's golden handbag and slung it over her shoulder. "I won't," she said.

"The van is here!" called Amma. Appa had organized an air-conditioned minivan to take them to the wedding hall so they wouldn't sweat in their best silk clothes.

Sona waved to Elephant through the window and the van drove off through the neighbouring streets to pick up Joy and Renu's families.

"One more stop," said Thatha, as the van stopped in front of Mullai's house.

"This is strange," Mullai said, when she got in. "I'm a passenger and not the driver."

Everyone laughed.

"Enjoy the ride," said Thatha. "We've got a *good* driver today."

"Hey! I'm a good driver," said Mullai. "Aren't I, girls?"

"Yes, you are!" shouted Sona, Joy and Renu. "The best driver in the whole world."

The wedding hall was busy. People milled about. Kids ran up and down the aisles.

Miss Rao was seated on the stage. She looked very different in a silk saree, her hair long with extensions, flowers and jewellery. There was a curtain and on the other side of the curtain, sat B-A-L-A-J-I. The groom.

"That's HIM," said Sona.

"He looks nice," said Joy.

"I don't like him," said Sona. "He's taking Miss Rao away from us."

Renu and Joy nodded. "We don't like him either," they chorused.

Amma led everyone towards the chairs where all the other school kids were seated with their parents.

"Come on," said Sona, "we must get everyone's names on the petition."

They passed the letter to each of their classmates to get their signatures.

"Are you all Sudha's students?" a lady asked.

"Who is Sudha?" asked Sona.

"Your teacher, the bride?"

"Oh, Miss Rao, our teacher," said Sona. "We never call her Sudha."

"Not 'Miss Rao' for long, is it?" said the woman as she went off to talk to someone else.

Sona gasped. She pulled Joy and Renu into a huddle. "Everyone knows that Miss Rao won't be our teacher any more!"

"Don't worry," said Renu. "We've done the petition. Surely she'll listen to us."

When everyone had signed the letter, Sona carefully put it in her bag and sat back to watch the wedding ceremony.

The wedding music grew louder.

"It's time for the Kanyadaanam ceremony," said Thatha. "This is the bit when your teacher actually gets married to Balaji."

Lots of people crowded around Miss Rao on one side of the curtain and the groom on the other. They couldn't see each other.

"Now the parents of Miss Rao are washing the feet of the groom to honour him," Thatha continued, pointing at the stage.

"Oh! It doesn't happen like that in Christian weddings," said Joy. "But the bride does wear a veil sometimes."

"Miss Rao's family have different customs, I think," said Thatha. "Look, now the groom is saying that he will always be by the bride's side in happiness and sorrow."

"Oh wow!" said Joy. "My cousin's husband said something like that in English during their wedding too."

"Because that's what good marriages are," said Thatha. "Like good friendships. You stick together no matter what."

Paatti leaned in and whispered, "Look, they are holding hands. It's happening."

Sona, Joy and Renu watched closely.

The priest chanted something in Sanskrit, an ancient Indian language. The groom then applied something on top of Miss Rao's head and then Miss Rao did the same on the groom's head.

"That's a mix of jaggery and cumin seeds," said Paatti. "The cumin is a symbol of bitterness and the jaggery is the symbol of sweetness."

"In bitterness and sweetness, we stick together," Thatha translated.

Sona looked at Joy and Renu. Uh-oh! If they stuck together, would Miss Rao live in Chennai without her husband?

The ceremony continued. Soon, the curtain was removed. The groom tied a yellow thread around Miss Rao's neck.

"And now they are really married," said Thatha.

Right after that, lots of people hurried to the stage to congratulate them.

"This is our chance," whispered Sona to her friends. "We must go to Miss Rao and hand over the petition."

"Now it's time for her family to wish her well," said Amma. "We can go at the end."

"We're family," said Sona. "We have to see her now."

Sona raced towards the stage with Renu and Joy right behind her.

"Hello, girls," said Miss Rao. "Thank you for coming."

"Congratulations," said Joy.

"Thank you," she said and turned to her new husband. "Balaji, this is Sona, this is Joy and this is Renu. They are the best of friends and the leaders of my class."

"Hello," said Balaji.

But Sona didn't reply. She just glared at him as if he was a movie villain.

"Congratulations," said Renu.

"Thanks," he said.

Sona knelt next to Miss Rao. "We have to give you something," she said, handing over the envelope with the petition.

"Aw! Thank you for the card," said Miss Rao, smiling.

Sona didn't correct her. Maybe Miss Rao wouldn't take the envelope if she knew it was a petition.

"Thank you, girls," said Miss Rao. "See you later."

Sona and her friends returned to their seats. Phew! They had done it. Everything was going to be OK. Miss Rao would read the petition and tell her husband that she wouldn't be moving to his city, after all.

Amma had said that fortune favours the brave. Sona had been brave – surely fortune would grant her wish now?

HOPING TO WIN

On Friday morning, Sona was still anxious about the petition. Monday was three full days away and Sona wanted to know right away if Miss Rao was leaving them or staying to be their teacher.

But Amma wouldn't let Sona hide in her room.

"Shall we play carrom?" she asked.

"No," said Sona. "You'll let me win."

"Playing board games is on your holiday list," Elephant reminded her.

"Come on, it'll be fun," said Amma. "How about you, me and Minmini against Thatha and Paatti?"

"We will win," said Thatha, bringing out the carrom board and placing it on the coffee table. "Your paatti was the state champion when she was in school."

"That was a long time ago," said Paatti, bringing the box of coins and the striker.

"I don't want to play," said Sona.

"Vaa!" said Minmini.

"Aw!" said Amma. "Minmini is calling you. She said 'vaa'."

"How did she know to say that?" asked Sona, smiling.

"She is learning words from her akka," said Thatha.

"You're Akka, the big sister," Elephant reminded her.

"I know," whispered

Sona, giving Minmini a kiss on the head.

"So shall we begin?" asked Thatha, opening the box of wooden coins.

Minmini giggled as the coins clattered onto the board. Then Paatti sprinkled some powder on the board to make the coins move faster. Sona and Minmini sat together facing Amma, their teammate. Thatha and Paatti faced each other, completing the other two sides of the square.

"Let's play the family points game," said Amma, stacking nine black coins on top of each other. Sona arranged the nine white coins next to them. Paatti balanced the red coin across the two tall stacks.

"Sona and Minmini, you go first," said Thatha. "Youngest first."

Sona pulled the round pink striker towards her. She aimed it at the stack of coins and flicked it with her fingers. It sailed across the board, scattering the coins.

Minmini clapped her hands and tried to jump on top of the board. Amma scooped her up quickly. As they played, Sona forgot all her worries about Miss Rao going away.

As the striker whizzed and the coins fell into the pockets, it was clear to Sona that Paatti and Thatha were winning.

"I'm going to lose," said Sona, eyeing her bounty and comparing it to Paatti's collection.

"I need some good luck."

"We don't need luck, Sona," said Amma. "We just have to play well. We can win if you pocket the red coin and follow it up with a black or a white."

"That's hard," said Sona. "Let me make a wish on my peacock feather first."

"All you need is focus," said Amma. "Trust me."

With Amma's guidance, Sona checked the angle of her striker and flicked it hard. The striker hit the red coin on the side and pushed it into the pocket. She jumped up and squealed.

Minmini clapped her hands. Sona started dancing and singing, "I'm going to win. I'm the winner."

"You still need to pocket a follow-through coin," Paatti reminded her.

This time Sona didn't wait to make a wish. She scanned

the board. There was one black coin and one white. The black coin was right next to the pocket. The white one was further away from the pocket, but its path was perfectly aligned.

"Both are possible," said Amma. "Which one do you want to try?"

Minmini pointed at the white one. Sona decided she would go for it, even if it was the harder option.

"Are you sure?" asked Amma, as she observed Sona lining up the shot.

"Yup!" said Sona.

"Fortune favours the brave," Elephant whispered.

Sona concentrated on the angle of strike, and thought back to Miss Rao's geometry lessons. She took a deep breath. Everyone was quiet. Even Minmini. *Even* Elephant.

Sona flicked the striker slowly, sending it across the board to tap the white coin with gentle force. The white coin sailed straight into the pocket.

"WE WON!" shouted Amma.

Sona hugged Amma and Minmini and Elephant.

"Congratulations on the win," said Paatti. "That was a really good shot."

"I think Sona takes after you!" said Thatha to Paatti.

That afternoon, as Sona played with Elephant and Minmini in the garden, something felt different. Winning the carrom game had made her feel hopeful.

"When you get older and go to school," said Sona to Minmini, "I hope Miss Rao will be your teacher too. She is the best teacher ever."

Minmini clapped her hands.

BESTEST FAREWELL

It was the weekend before Sona and her friends had to go back to school. On Saturday morning, Sona called a meeting.

"I don't want to go to school on Monday," said Sona. "I will never step inside our classroom without Miss Rao being our teacher."

"I don't want to miss school," said Joy.

"I'm not sure my mum will let me skip school," said Renu.

"Not sure your amma will let you either!" said Elephant to Sona.

KNOCK-KNOCK!

Appa peeped his head in. "Girls, please can I come in?" he said. "I've something to show you."

"What is it?" asked Sona, a little bit of impatience in her voice. "We are having a meeting about Miss Rao."

"Actually, it's sort of related to that," said Appa, coming in and sitting on the bed. He pulled out a bundle of things from a cloth bag. Sona and her friends gathered around excitedly.

"This is my end of year photo," he said, taking a picture from the pile, "from when I was finishing fifth standard and moving on to secondary school."

Me and my Teachers

"You look silly," said Sona.

"I don't look silly, just goofy," said Appa. "Look, these are my teachers. I didn't want to leave them and go to a new secondary school for sixth standard."

"Were you sad?" asked Sona. She couldn't imagine leaving behind *all* her teachers, not just Miss Rao.

"A little bit," said Appa. "I was worried the new teachers wouldn't like me, or would be too strict, or wouldn't understand how much I loved computers and not art."

"I love art," said Sona.

"We all like different things, don't we?" said Appa.

"What happened at your new school?" asked Joy.

Appa smiled and pulled out another photo, this time from his sixth standard. "I needn't have worried," he said. "My new teachers were amazing. In fact, one of them taught me how I could become a software engineer."

"But what happened to your old teachers?" asked Renu.

"I kept in touch with most of my teachers," Appa said. He pulled a photo album from the pile and showed them recent pictures he had taken at his old school. "I still go back there to talk to the students once in a while."

Sona flipped through the album. "You still look goofy," she said.

Appa laughed and opened a small notebook.

"What's this?" asked Sona.

"It's an autograph book," he said. "Everyone in my class signed it at the end of each year when we moved to the next class – the teachers too. Let me read my teachers' messages.

"*'Dear Raghunath, always be cheerful.'*

"*'Dear Raghu, always shine through.'*

"*'Dear Raghunath, follow your heart.'*"

Sona sat by the bed and flipped through the autograph book.

"It's not the same though, is it?" asked Sona. "*We're* not leaving; our teacher is."

"Sona," said Appa gently. "If Miss Rao is leaving, we can still keep in touch with her. Maybe she will visit the school every time she comes back to this city. But what's most important is to remember everything she has taught you and to make her proud."

"Did you make your teachers proud?" asked Joy.

"I hope so," said Appa. "Next time I visit my school, I'll take you with me and you can ask!"

Sona giggled. "That will be fun," she said. "What if they tell me you were very naughty?"

"That would be a lie," said Appa, laughing.

"I don't remember being naughty at all."

"I remember," a voice said. Paatti came in with a bowl full of fruit and a jug of juice for everyone. "You were so naughty that I had to go in once a month to apologize to your teachers."

Paatti told them some stories about Appa in school which made them giggle and laugh. After Paatti left, Appa packed up his things and sighed.

"Sona," he said gently, "and Joy and Renu, let me tell you one last thing. It's a lot more fun to be excited about what's happening than to be disappointed about what's *not* happening."

After Appa left the room, Sona sighed loudly.

"I think Appa is telling us that we should be excited about whoever our new teacher is, instead of missing Miss Rao so much," said Sona.

"If the jaggery and cumin thing at the wedding worked, Miss Rao will never leave her husband's side, right?"

"We can't stop Miss Rao from going to Vijayawada, can we?" said Joy.

"What should we do then?" asked Renu.

"The President told me the other day that she let Uncle Prasad go abroad even though she didn't want him to. Because she loved him so much."

"So, you think we should let Miss Rao go, even though we love her?" asked Renu.

"*Because* we love her," said Joy. "We don't want her to stay if that's going to make her sad."

Sona nodded. "That's what Amma said about Mullai," said Sona. "When they were girls and Mullai didn't want to sing, Amma didn't force her. That's why they are still friends today."

"I want to be friends with Miss Rao for ever," said Joy.

No one said anything after that, for a long time. Elephant jumped off the bed and rolled on the floor to make them laugh, but Sona didn't even pick him up.

"I think we must send our best wishes to Miss Rao," said Sona.

"There is one problem though," said Joy. "We already gave her our petition."

"Maybe she hasn't opened it yet," said Renu.

"OK, let's make farewell cards," said Sona, "*bursting* with all our best wishes."

And so, for the rest of the afternoon, Sona and her friends worked on a card each.

Sona drew Elephant on hers. The card read, "*We will miss you. But we wish you a trumpeting time.*"

"That's funny," said Renu. I wrote 'You're the bestest teacher in the whole world and come back to see us soon.'"

"She's going to correct your English and say 'bestest' is not a word," said Joy and giggled.

Joy had written her card on behalf of the whole class. She was always thinking like a class leader, thought Sona.

"Dear Miss Rao, ♡ ♡ ♡
Thank you for being our teacher ever since we were little. We hope you will be happy teaching other children in your new city. They are lucky! But we are lucky too, because we had you as our teacher for three years. We will miss you and please come back soon."

Sona's eyes teared up at the thought of Miss Rao teaching other children. But it was like Appa said: they had to let Miss Rao go.

That night, after Amma and Appa had kissed

her goodnight, Sona lay quietly in her bed, with Elephant next to her on her pillow.

"Sona," whispered Elephant. "Your tears are making me wet."

"Sorry," said Sona. "I can't seem to stop them."

"When Elephants can't stop crying, they ask the shadows of the night to bring them sleep," said Elephant. "I read that somewhere."

"You can't read," said Sona, with a little giggle.

Hugging Elephant tight, Sona looked through the window and whispered to the shadows to bring her sleep.

All Change!

On their way to school on Monday morning, Sona, Joy and Renu were quiet. They held hands in the back of the auto-rickshaw, but didn't say anything. They didn't need to.

"What's wrong with you three?" asked Mullai. "Forgot to do your holiday homework?"

"Nothing," said Joy.

"Uh-oh!" said Mullai. "Are you worried Miss Rao won't be back from her honeymoon?"

95

"Honey-what?" asked Renu.

"Out of town holiday," said Mullai. "After a wedding."

"We're worried she's not coming back at all," said Sona.

"Uh-oh!" said Mullai. "That is serious. Did you give her a farewell card at the wedding then? I saw you all signing something."

Mullai never missed anything, thought Sona.

"We gave her a petition," said Joy. "To ask her not to leave our school to live somewhere else with her husband."

"Ouch!" said Mullai. "That's harsh. Do you think that would be right?"

"Not really," said Sona. "That's why we made her farewell cards over the weekend instead. We're going to give them to the principal, and ask her to send them on to Miss Rao, with all our love and good wishes."

"That's good," said Mullai. "Miss Rao was a lovely teacher."

Sona, Joy and Renu ran to their classroom, dropped their bags and headed towards the staff room.

"Maybe we can quickly peep in to see if there's a new teacher there," said Sona. "*Our* new teacher."

SWISH! The doors opened.

Mrs Girija Shekar, their principal, walked out of the staff room.

"Good morning, Mrs Shekar," said Sona.

"Hey, Sona! There you are, Joy and Renu," she said. "I was looking for the three of you."

Sona was aghast. She looked at Joy and Renu. Joy shook her head.

"Us? Why?" asked Sona.

"I wanted to commend you on your joint letter," said Mrs Shekar. "It was well written. And it's a great way to learn how to organize a group of people to sign something."

Joy's mouth fell open. Renu was looking for spots on her shoes.

"You mean the petition?" asked Sona.

"But how did *you* read it, Miss?" asked Joy.

"Your teacher showed it to me," said their principal curtly, "because she was so impressed."

"We're sorry now that we wrote it," said Sona. "We shouldn't have asked Miss Rao to stay if she wanted to leave."

Mrs Shekar folded her arms across her chest and sighed loudly.

"That's right," she said. "But Miss Rao probably didn't mind because she knows how much you love her. Try to petition for positive things next time."

Sona couldn't look up into Mrs Shekar's eyes. She just nodded solemnly. Renu reached for Sona's hand.

"We brought farewell cards for Miss Rao," said Joy.

Joy always knew the right thing to say, thought Sona.

TRRRRRRING!

"Well, it's time for class now," said Mrs Shekar. "Give them to your teacher."

"It's not Miss Rao, is it?" asked Joy, looking at Sona.

"That would be impossible," said Mrs Shekar. "Of course it's not Miss Rao any more."

Sona's eyes filled with tears, even though she had meant every word in her farewell card and she had been expecting to meet a new teacher.

Mrs Shekar's face softened. She put an arm around Sona. "Hey, hey! As long as you learn from your mistakes, there's nothing to cry about."

Sona shook her head. Joy and Renu held Sona's hand to comfort her, their eyes brimming with tears too.

"Come on, I'll take you to your class."

When they entered their class, Sona didn't even look up. Joy gasped. Renu tugged Sona's hand.

"There you are," said a familiar voice. "I was just wondering what had happened to the amazing letter writers."

Sona looked up in surprise. It was Miss Rao.

"But you just said our teacher *wasn't* Miss Rao?" demanded Sona, turning to Mrs Shekar.

"Oh! I'm sorry," said Mrs Shekar. "Did you think you had a *new* teacher? I simply meant that Miss Rao is no longer 'Miss Rao'. She changed her name; she is now Mrs Sudha Balaji."

"But she *is* Miss Rao," wailed Sona, giggles trying to break out through her tears.

"But she got married," said Mrs Shekar, gently.

"'Miss' is used for women who are not married," Joy explained.

"That's right," said Mrs Balaji.

Sona rushed to Mrs Balaji and hugged her. "Why didn't you tell us you weren't leaving?" she asked.

"Because I was *never* leaving," said Mrs Balaji. "Don't you think I would have told you all if I was leaving?"

"We were *so* worried," said Joy. "We thought you were going to Vijayawada."

"Nope!"

"But how will you see your husband then?" asked Renu. "He'll be so far away."

"My husband works in this city too," Mrs Balaji explained. "So, I'm not leaving the city, or the school, or your class."

Sona sighed deeply. She had worried for nine whole days for nothing. They had searched for lucky objects and made wishes. They had written a petition and made farewell cards, and Miss Rao wasn't even going anywhere! Sona felt a bit silly that she had panicked and worried her friends too.

"But why didn't you tell us that, after you saw the petition?"

"I'm sorry, Sona. I had no idea you were all

so concerned," said Mrs Balaji. "I only opened your letter this morning, and then I showed it to Mrs Shekar because I wanted her to know how much you love being in my class," said Mrs Balaji. "But more importantly, I wanted her to see how good your letter was and how clever you were to get it signed by all your class. I've taught you well, haven't I?"

"That's why we want you to be our teacher for ever and ever!" said Sona.

Mrs Shekar held out the farewell cards Sona had handed to her earlier. "Here, they have written you *more* letters!"

"No!" Sona screeched. She pounced forward and grabbed the cards from Mrs Shekar's hands. "These cards are not for you, Mrs Balaji. They were meant for Miss Rao!"

"All right then," said Mrs Balaji, with a chuckle. "Back to your seats because we still have things to study – and you're stuck with me."

"No chance," said Pradeep. "We have so many wedding questions for you."

"What was the best present you got?" someone asked.

"She didn't want any presents," said Sona. "That made us very suspicious."

"You'll make good detectives," said Mrs Balaji.

"Right, everyone, I need to talk to you about something important."

This sounded serious. Everyone settled down quickly and hushed.

"Thank you all for coming to my wedding," said Mrs Balaji. "It was lovely to see you all there to wish me well."

"And to sign the petition," said Pradeep, loudly.

"Yes, I'm coming to that," said Mrs Balaji. "I'm very happy that you want to be in my class for ever and ever. I'm also proud that you wrote a petition and collected signatures from everyone."

"There is a 'but' coming," whispered Joy.

"But..." said Mrs Balaji, "you needn't have worried. In all that worrying, you forgot one important thing. Would I *ever* go away without saying goodbye? Of course I would have told you if you were getting a new teacher."

Sona nodded. She should have known that.

She raised her hand.

"I'm sorry, Miss Rao ... *Mrs Balaji*," she said. "I was the one who panicked everyone. But yesterday – after a long chat with Appa and Paatti – Joy, Renu and I realized we were wrong to write the petition."

Mrs Balaji nodded with a quiet smile.

"We shouldn't have tried to stop you," continued Sona. "It was wrong of us."

"Thank you, girls," said Mrs Balaji. "You're very brave to explain this to the class. But even if I was leaving, you shouldn't be afraid of getting a new teacher. Change is a good thing – it's how we learn and grow and flourish. Even if you feel sad about it in the beginning, it might turn out to be the best thing that ever happens to you."

And so that was that. Miss Rao was back. But she was Mrs Balaji now. She was the same, but a little bit changed; and *that* was a good thing.

At bedtime, Sona lay in bed thinking about what Mrs Balaji had taught them that day. Sona didn't want to be afraid of change. She wanted to learn and grow and flourish.

"As long as I can be next to you, growing and flourishing too," said Elephant.

Sona hugged Elephant. "That's not going to change," she whispered.

"That's good then," said Elephant. "Goodnight."

"Goodnight," whispered Sona.

NEW WORDS TO EXPLORE IN THIS STORY

akka – big sister.

chutney – chutney is a dipping sauce made with different ingredients.

idli – steamed rice cake made with a fermented mix of rice and lentil batter.

Kanyadaanam – the ceremony in which a father gives away his daughter in marriage; "kanya" means "daughter" and "daanam" means "give away".

muhurtham – an auspicious time to perform a ceremony.

murukku – a spirally, crispy snack made of lentil flour.

sambhar – a lentil and tamarind dish that is perfect to eat with steamed rice.

Sanskrit – an ancient Indian language.

Tamil – the language spoken by Sona and her family.

tiffin – a light meal usually eaten between lunch and dinner.

vaa – the Tamil word to beckon or welcome or call.

COLLECT ALL THE
SONA SHARMA BOOKS:

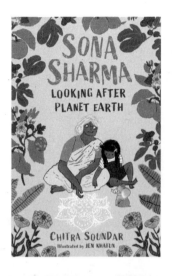

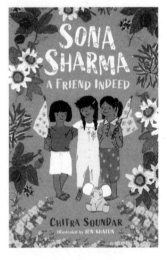

ALSO BY CHITRA SOUNDAR:

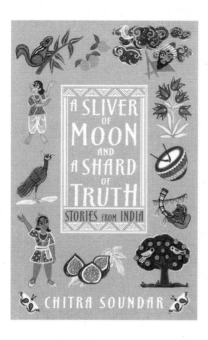

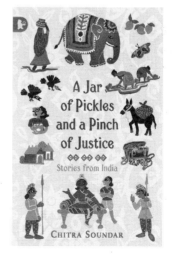

Chitra Soundar is originally from the culturally colourful India, where traditions, festivals and mythology are a way of life. As a child, she feasted on generous portions of folktales and stories from Hindu mythology. As she grew older, she started making up her own stories. Chitra now lives in London, cramming her little flat with story books and lucky charms of all kinds.

Jen Khatun's work is inspired by the natural world, the books on her shelves and the hidden magical moments found in everyday life. She says, "Being of Bangladeshi heritage means that Chitra's stories remind me of the close bonds, traditions and memories of my family life. As a grown-up, I cherish every profound life-teaching my family gifted me; they have made me who I am today."